W9-AGK-595

A Very Special Tea Party

Based on the stories by Katharine Holabird
Based on the illustrations by Helen Craig

Grosset & Dunlap
An Imprint of Penguin Group (USA) Inc.

Angelina Ballerina © 2007 Helen Craig Ltd. (illustrations) and Katharine Holabird (text). The Angelina Ballerina name and character and the dancing Angelina logo are trademarks of HIT Entertainment Limited, Katharine Holabird and Helen Craig Ltd., Reg. U.S. Pat. & Tm. Off. Used under license by Penguin Young Readers Group. All rights reserved. Published by Grosset & Dunlap, a division of Penguin Young Readers Group, 345 Hudson Street, New York, New York 10014. GROSSET & DUNLAP is a trademark of Penguin Group (USA) Inc. Manufactured in China.

ISBN 978-0-448-44549-6   1 0 9 8 7 6 5

Alice's birthday is almost here. Angelina is throwing a surprise tea party for her. Angelina invites all their friends.

Use the stickers to decorate Angelina's desk and help make Alice's birthday invitations.

Angelina goes to Mrs. Thimble's shop to get decorations and treats for the party.

Help Angelina pick out items for the party.

Angelina and Mrs. Mouseling make Alice's favorite cakes and cookies for her special day.

Use the stickers to help Mrs. Mouseling and Angelina make goodies for Alice.

On the morning of her birthday, Alice comes over bright and early. Angelina pretends she has chores to do. Angelina tells Alice that she cannot play. "Come back around four o'clock and we'll practice our pirouettes."

Alice is very sad—she thinks that Angelina has forgotten her birthday.

Use the stickers to decorate the scene.

Later that afternoon, the guests arrive for the party.
"Where's Alice?" asks Henry.
"She'll be here soon," replies Angelina. "She's in for a
very big surprise."

Use the stickers to decorate for Alice's surprise tea party.

Use the stickers to show Alice arriving at the party.

At four o'clock, Alice comes back to Angelina's house. "Hello?" she calls. It looks as if no one is home!

All of a sudden, her friends jump out from their hiding places and yell, "Surprise!"

"Oh, my!" exclaims Alice. "I thought everyone had forgotten my birthday!"

Soon, it is time for Alice's birthday cake. She makes a wish and blows out the candles. "This was the best birthday ever!" Alice exclaims.

Use the stickers to decorate Alice's cake.

After the party, Angelina and Alice are very happy and very tired.
"Thank you so much, Angelina," says Alice. "You are the best
friend a mouseling could ask for."
"And so are you," Angelina tells Alice. "Happy birthday!"

Use the stickers to decorate Angelina's bedroom.

Use these stickers
on pages 2–3

Surprise
Tea Party
for
Alice's birthday
Angelina's house
3 pm

Use these stickers
on pages 4–5

© 2007 Helen Craig Ltd. and Katharine Holabird

Use these stickers
on pages 6–7

Use these stickers
on pages 8–9

© 2007 Helen Craig Ltd. and Katharine Holabird

Use these stickers on pages 10–11

Use these stickers on pages 12–13

© 2007 Helen Craig Ltd. and Katharine Holabird

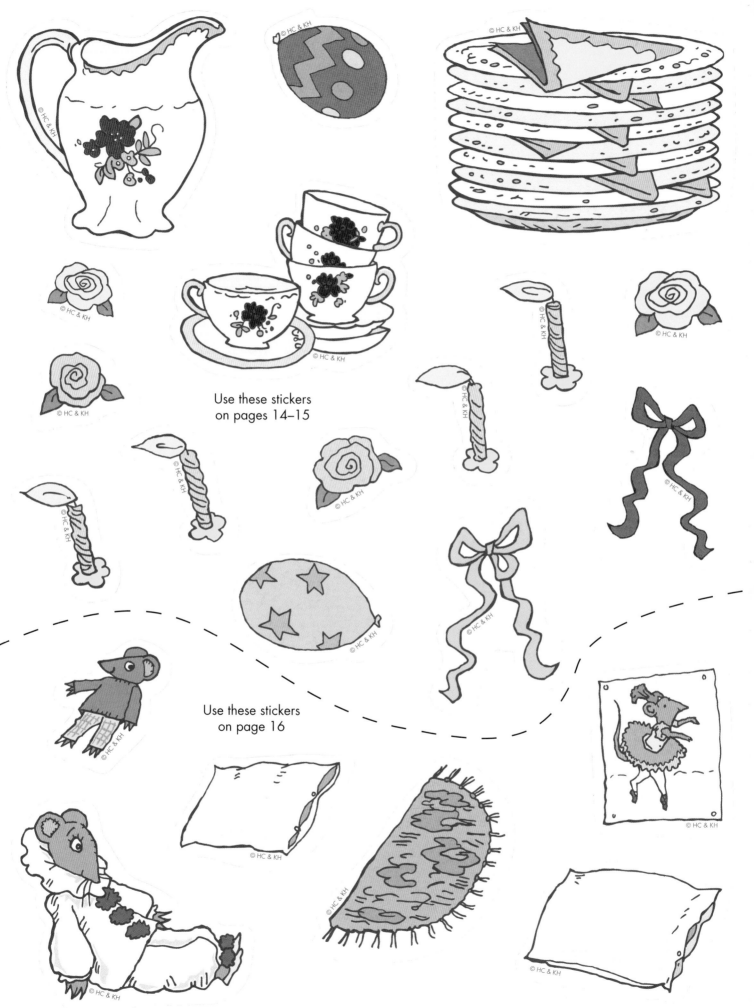

Use these stickers
on pages 14–15

Use these stickers
on page 16

© 2007 Helen Craig Ltd. and Katharine Holabird